Best Friends

By ALLISON DAVIS
Illustrated by DAVID PREBENNA

A SESAME STREET / GOLDEN PRESS BOOK

Published by Western Publishing Company, Inc., in conjunction with Children's Television Workshop.

B.BIRD

SNUFFY

ERNIE

BERT

Big Bird and Snuffy were best friends. They played together every morning at preschool. They played pretend with puppets.

They played the piano.

They solved puzzles...

and they solved mysteries.

When it was time to play dress-up, Snuffy and
Big Bird always dressed the same.

"Howdy, pardner," Big Bird would holler to his friend
as he galloped by.

"Howdy, pardner," Snuffy would drawl, tipping his
ten-gallon hat.

When it was time to line up to go out to the playground, they were partners then, too.

Big Bird and Snuffy always sat
side by side for storytime.

They traded snacks...

and they
traded secrets.

One day, when everyone was lining up to go outside,
Ernie ran up to Snuffy and said, "Let's be partners!"
"Okay," said Snuffy.
Big Bird had no partner. He had to go to the end of
the line and be partners with Ethel, the teacher.

Outside, Big Bird ran to push Snuffy on the swing, but Snuffy said, "I don't need a push, Bird. Ernie is teaching me how to pump! Watch this!" Snuffy stretched his legs out straight when he swung forward and bent his knees when he swung back.

"Swing with us, Big Bird," said Ernie. But Big Bird didn't feel like swinging anymore.

Big Bird looked around the playground. Everyone else was busy. There was no one to play with.

He trudged back to the steps and sat down. Big Bird didn't even hear Bert ask him if he wanted to play.

At storytime, Big Bird tried to sit next to Snuffy, but he couldn't. Ernie was already sitting on one side. Herry was on the other. Big Bird tried to schooch up close behind Snuffy, but he sat on Herry's finger by mistake.

"Owww!" Herry cried.

"Big Bird, dear," said Ethel, "would you please sit back a little? Thank you."

Big Bird felt like he was going to cry.

"Hi, Bird," said Snuffy as he sat down beside him at
snacktime. "Trade you my crackers for your carrots."

"No, thanks," said Big Bird.

"I'll trade you my apple for your crackers, Snuffy,"
said Ernie, sliding in beside them.

"Okay," said Snuffy.

Then it was time to go home, and the grown-ups
arrived. As Snuffy was leaving, Ernie ran up with a
picture he had painted. Big Bird thought it was the
most beautiful picture of Snuffy he had ever seen. It
had pretty orange flecks in it, just the way Snuffy's fur
did.

"'To Snuffy, from your friend Ernie,'" read
Mrs. Snuffleupagus.

TO
SNUFFY,
FROM YOUR
FRIEND ERNIE

Big Bird burst out the door, and Granny had to hurry
to catch up with him. "Wait for me, dearie," she said.
"Why, Big Bird, what's wrong?"

Big Bird leaned against her shoulder and cried and
cried. "Snuffy isn't my friend anymore," he sobbed. "He's
Ernie's friend." Then he told Granny everything that
had happened.

"It's hard to share a friend," said Granny. "But Snuffy can be your friend *and* Ernie's friend. Some things are more fun with three. It just depends."

HONK! HONK! Snuffy and his mommy drove by and waved. "Bye, Bird," called Snuffy. "See you tomorrow, buddy." Granny looked over at Big Bird and smiled.

The next day, Big Bird and Snuffy put on a
puppet show. But this time they had someone
to watch the show.

When they went out to play,
Ernie and Snuffy showed
Big Bird how to pump.

"Whee!" yelled Big Bird. "This
is fun!"

Now at storytime, Big Bird sits on one side of Snuffy and Ernie sits on the other.

And at snacktime, Big Bird and Snuffy and Ernie all share.

It's just as Granny said: Some things are more fun when there are three...

or four...

or more!

It just depends.